D1643646

Luna the Little Ghost

Story by Jana Novotny Hunter
Pictures by Sue Porter

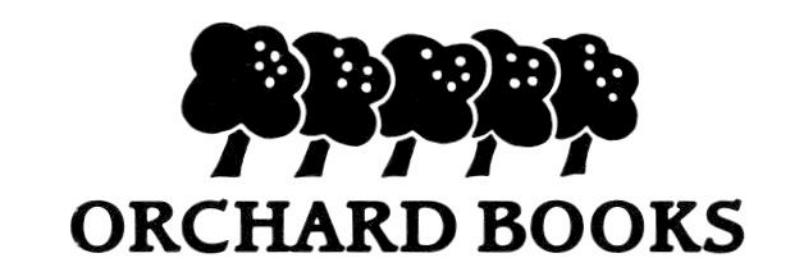

ORCHARD BOOKS

Designed by Sue Porter for Orchard Books

First published in Great Britain in 1991 by
ORCHARD BOOKS
96 Leonard Street, London EC2A 4RH
Orchard Books Australia
14 Mars Road, Lane Cove NSW 2066
1 85213 270 1
A CIP catalogue record for this book
is available from the British Library.
Printed in Belgium

In the churchyard it is dusky night. Rosy mists cloud the moon. Bats swoop in the shadows. Silent and soft, a shape drifts across the graves . . . Searching.

The shape hovers.

"Whoooooo. . . ?" it moans.

It is a silvery shape. Sometimes it stretches, long and thin, like steam.

Sometimes it shrinks to raindrop size. Then it bounces around the churchyard, like a raindrop bubble.

What is this silvery shape?
And why does it search?
Is it steam?
Is it a raindrop?
Is it a bubble?

No! It's . . .

. . . A ghost!

Luna, the little ghost.

Mischievous Luna,
full of spooky fun,
silvery Luna,
playful as a bubble,
are you searching
for a playmate tonight?

Little Luna does not speak. She dances around the churchyard. She hides behind a headstone, then out she peeps.

"*Yes!*"

She drifts across the churchyard, to the shadowy farm.

She fades . . . then takes shape again. And floats to a moonlit barn.

"Whoooooo . . . ?" Luna moans as a giant shadow looms.

"Whooo-hooo . . . ?"
Luna hoots as the cow waves her tail.
"**Moo, moo**!" bellows the cow.
Luna backs away. "Boo-hoooooo,"
she seems to say as she floats off
towards the little house, the little
wooden house where . . .

. . . the dog dozes.

Luna hovers, spins, then suddenly swoops.

"Aaoooo!" the dog howls, backing inside his kennel.

"Grrraaooooo!" he growls.
"Boo-hooo . . ." Luna seems
to howl as she drifts away.

She floats towards the big house, the house near the moonlit barn. The house the dog guards.
"Whoooooo . . . !" Luna moans.

She peers through the window to the hallway, where shadows stretch like fingers.

No one stirs.

“Whoooooo . . . ?” Luna wails.
Light as a bubble, she fades through
the wall.

Silent and soft, she floats up, up the stairs . . .

. . . into a room . . . a cosy room . . .

. . . where a child sleeps.

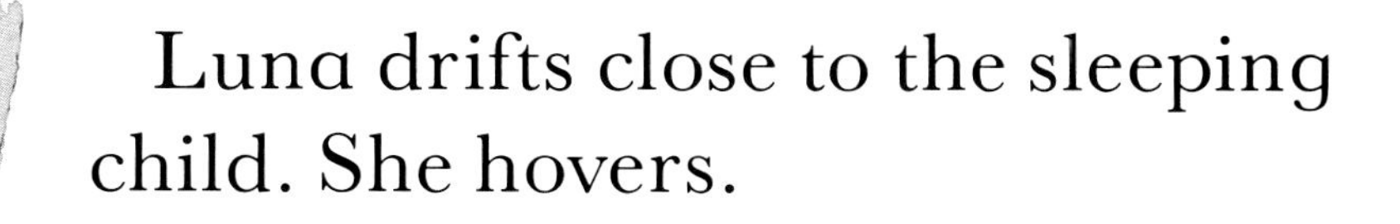

Luna drifts close to the sleeping child. She hovers.

The child shivers, stirs, awakes, and rubs sleepy eyes.

"Little ghost? Little ghost, is that you?"
Luna shimmers, "Y-e-e-e-s."

"Little ghost, what do you want?"
asks the child.
"Ooo-ooo," Luna flaps and spins.
"Oooo-ooo-oo." She circles the ceiling
and dances about.
"Little ghost, do you want . . . some
spooky fun?"

Luna, excited, shimmers, "Y-e-e-e-s."
The child smiles. "Spooky, scary, midnight fun?"
"*Whoo-hoo!*" Luna hoots, flapping for joy. She circles the ceiling and spins around, making shadows loom.

The child hides under sheets . . . makes shadows loom . . . and dances for joy on the bed.

"*Yaay!*"

Luna, bright as quicksilver, full of spooky fun, scoots under sheets . . . zooms across the room! Dances on the ceiling!

Together, touched by magic, they ride a moonlit breeze, to whoop and tumble full of fun . . .
. . . above the shadowy trees.

Tumbling over and under they fly, little ghost and child. Twirling, whirling, two spinning raindrop bubbles, shimmering and wild!

wheeeee!

Little Luna and the child play ghost games all through the night . . . joined by creatures no longer afraid, till dawn spreads a misty light.

Then back, back they fly. Back to the house to the cosy room . . . where the little bed lies waiting.

The child cuddles and snuggles, as
Luna flutters goodbye.
"Oooooo-ooooo . . ."

Shimmering, she floats back to her churchyard.

Tomorrow she will search again. Softly, silently, she will drift... searching for spooky fun.

Someone to play with in the mist . . .

Maybe you'll be the one!